Little Sparkles

Party on the Pirate Ship

Collect all the

LITTLE SPARKLES

Little Sparkles

Party on the Pirate Ship

Emily Moon

SCHOLASTIC

First published in the UK in 2012 by Scholastic Children's Books
An imprint of Scholastic Ltd
Euston House, 24 Eversholt Street
London, NW1 1DB, UK
Registered office: Westfield Road, Southam, Warwickshire, CV47 0RA
SCHOLASTIC and associated logos are trademarks and/or
registered trademarks of Scholastic Inc.
Series created by Working Partners Ltd.

Text copyright © Working Partners Ltd., 2012
Illustration copyright © Dynamo, 2012

ISBN 978 1407 12459 9

Printed and bound by CPI Group (UK) Ltd., Croydon, CR0 4YY
Papers used by Scholastic Children's Books
are made from wood grown in sustainable forests.

1 3 5 7 9 10 8 6 4 2

This is a work of fiction. Names, characters, places,
incidents and dialogues are products of the author's imagination
or are used fictitiously. Any resemblance to actual people, living
or dead, events or locales is entirely coincidental.

www.scholastic.co.uk/zone

With special thanks to Jane Clarke

For Helen and Amy, welcome aboard!

Dear Holly + Rose,

Yo-ho-ho!

All aboard the Jolly Roger for my birthday party!

It's on Saturday at 2 o'clock at the Adventure Park.

Please come in pirate fancy dress.

Love

Captain Hari of the High Seas

1

Yo-Ho-Ho, Off to the Party We Go!

"Yo-ho-ho! A pirate's life for me!" sang Holly and Rose as they skipped hand in hand up to the entrance of the Adventure Park. The twins couldn't wait to get to Hari's pirate party. His mum had booked the Jolly Roger Pirate Ship ride for the whole afternoon!

"Arrr!" Holly growled. The twins were wearing fancy dress, and she stamped her boots and made her long red skirt swing as she skipped. "I'm Swashbuckling Holly! Swashbuckling Holly will make you swab the decks!"

Rose's baggy red trousers swished as she stomped her boots.

"Narrr!" she retorted. "Peg Leg Rose will make you walk the plank first!"

The twins shared a giggle. Their long toffee-coloured plaits bounced beneath their pirates' hats as they skipped past the teacup ride and the carousel, waving at the happy children who whizzed round on them.

"Yo-ho-ho! This party is going to be fun!" Holly laughed.

"Especially if the Little Sparkles turn

up!" Rose said, so excited at the thought that she forgot to pretend to be a pirate.

"I really, really hope they do!" exclaimed Holly.

They'd already had three amazing adventures with the five tiny magical creatures who were the Little Sparkles. Each time, they'd helped them stop the nasty Party Poopers spoiling things for everyone.

"But if the Little Sparkles come to Hari's party, the Poopers might, too – and we're the only people who can see them. It's up to us to stop them ruining everything," Rose reminded Holly.

"Arrrr! Party Poopers are scallywags!"

Holly declared. "But if they try to scupper the Jolly Roger, Swashbuckling Holly and Peg Leg Rose will save the day!"

They stopped in front of a life-size wooden pirate ship with a big canvas sail and a skull-and-crossbones flag on top of the crow's nest. It was raised off the ground on a giant mechanical swing that made it sway gently, like it was at sea.

"Ahoy there!" Hari yelled down from the deck. "Come aboard, me hearties!" he commanded, waving his pirate hat in the air.

"Aye, aye, Captain Hari of the High Seas!" Holly and Rose called. They raced

across the rope bridge on to the deck. The
Jolly Roger was decorated with fluttering
red and black flags. Orange, green and

yellow balloons in the shape of parrots were tied on to the mast and railings. It was fabulous!

"Happy birthday, Hari!" Holly and Rose said together. Holly gave Hari the present she was carrying. "It's from both of us," she explained.

"Thanks very much!" said Hari.

His eyes gleamed as he lifted his eyepatch. He squeezed his gift through its brightly coloured wrapping paper, like he was trying to work out what it was; then he handed it to his mum. She put it with the others on a table at the side of the ship.

"Come and join the crew!" Hari said.

Jenny, Billy, Maisie and the other pirate party guests were gathered around a big table covered in an ocean-blue tablecloth. The plates of food were decorated with mini plastic palm trees.

"They look like treasure islands on the sea!" Holly breathed.

There was an island of cheese and pineapple squares skewered with tiny plastic cutlasses, and an island of cupcakes in black paper cases, decorated with a skull-and-crossbones. On the biggest island, there was a birthday cake in the shape of a treasure chest, coated with thick chocolate icing and surrounded by sweets and gold-wrapped chocolate coins.

"Yummy!" Rose murmured.

"And there's a pirate keg for drink!" Jenny laughed, indicating a big barrel with "Lemonade" painted on the side.

The sun shone down on the Jolly

Roger, and the flags fluttered and the parrot balloons swayed in the soft breeze created by the movement of the ship.

"It feels like we are sailing off on a pirate adventure!" Maisie giggled.

Rose and Holly glanced round at their friends' happy smiling faces.

"It's perfect," Rose said.

"Everyone's here!" Hari's mum announced. "It's time for Captain Hari's pirate party to get going!"

But as soon as the words were out of her mouth, there was a CREAK and the Jolly Roger went still.

Holly and Rose looked at each other.

Each twin knew what the other was

thinking. Could this be the work of the Party Poopers?

2

A Surprise in the Crow's Nest

"The Jolly Roger's stopped moving!" Hari cried.

Rose and Holly looked at each other. They couldn't let the Poopers spoil Hari's day!

"Never mind, Hari," said Rose, thinking fast. "It will make it ... um ... easier to climb up to the crow's nest."

"And we can still steer the ship's wheel," Holly added.

Hari looked more cheerful. "We can walk the plank, too!" he said, leading the way to a wooden beam that hung off the edge of the ship.

The Jolly Roger rang with cries of "Yo-ho-ho!" and "Shiver me timbers!" as the

children in their pirate costumes took it in turns to walk the plank, jumping off on to the soft mat on the ground below.

"Whenever the Party Poopers are spoiling things, the Little Sparkles are usually close by," Rose whispered to Holly. "Can you see them?"

She shaded her eyes against the sun and looked round the ship. Holly did the same. She could see something shimmering around the top of the mast.

"Up there," Holly whispered. "In the crow's nest. Come on!"

The twins excitedly climbed up the rope netting towards the circular platform fixed around the top of the

Jolly Roger's mast. As they got closer a tinkling noise like tiny wind chimes filled the air and brightly coloured glitter sprinkled down on their pirate hats.

"The Little Sparkles *are* here!" Rose exclaimed happily.

Bobbing up and down inside the safety net around the crow's nest were the five fluffy, magical animals, each carrying a miniature party bag. Princess the pony pranced in delight when she saw the twins, Tikki the tiny yellow kitten purred and purred, and Peppy the puppy wagged his tail in a sparkle of light-blue glitter. Bubbles the pink bunny hopped on to Rose's shoulder.

"Bubbles thinks she's a pirate's parrot," Tubbs the turtle joked, doing a head-over-heels roll so that his rainbow shell shimmered in the sunshine.

"We are so happy to see you!" Holly told the tiny creatures as she and Rose squeezed into the crow's nest and stood beside a telescope mounted on a stand. "But where are the Poopers? We have to stop them from making anything else go wrong – and turn them into Little Sparkles!"

The twins had discovered that if they could make the Party Poopers have fun, they changed into new Little Sparkles. They had already transformed three

Poopers into a chick, a guinea pig and a seahorse.

"Maybe I can spy them through this," said Rose.

She put her eye to the telescope and tilted it so she could see down over the deck. The walk-the-plank game had ended and Hari's mum and the party guests were gathered around the Jolly Roger's steering wheel.

Rose focused the telescope on the party table.

"Oh no!" she gasped as the plates of cupcakes and the cheese and pineapple nibbles tipped over and the treasure chest birthday cake splattered across the ocean-blue cloth. "Those nasty Poopers are messing up the food. Quick, we have to get down there!"

Bubbles hopped off Rose's shoulder as she and Holly scrambled back down the netting and on to the deck. The Little Sparkles floated down and hovered beside them in a shimmering cloud.

There, on the tabletop, standing right in the middle of the splattered birthday cake,

was one of the two remaining Party Poopers. His blobby grey body was all covered in chocolate icing and a skull-and-crossbones cupcake case was stuck to his head.

He stuck out his tongue.

"Ner, ner!" he said, leaping off the table.

The second Pooper stopped kicking a cube of cheese and screwed up his frowny grey face.

"It's those smiley niceys and those pesky girls again!" he grumbled. "The ones that think parties should be fun!"

"Well, this is what Party Poopers think," the previous Pooper shouted, stomping his stubby feet so that pieces of cheese and pineapple and icing showered across the table. "Parties are rubbish – parties stink!"

The two Poopers gave each other a high five and with a blobbety-blob, they leapt on the present table and grabbed hold of the gift Holly and Rose had given to Hari.

"Bye byeeee! We're going to put this present where you'll never find it!" the Poopers yelled as they bounded over the side. The twins could hear a SPLAT as the Poopers landed on the path beside the pirate ship.

"We have to get Hari's present back!" Holly cried, racing towards the plank.

3

Hunting for Treasure

Holly and Rose raced along the wobbly plank and leaped off the end.

WHUMP! They landed on the mat below. There was a zippety-zappety flash as the Little Sparkles whizzed to where the Poopers had jumped off the Jolly Roger. Holly and Rose raced round to join them.

In the spot where the Poopers had landed was a blob of chocolate icing and a line of sticky little footprints leading away from it.

Tikki patted them gently with her tiny yellow paw, and gave a small meow. She sang softly:

"*Silly old Poopers left a track,*
Now we can get the present back."

Peppy sniffed curiously at the prints. Then, as Tikki's song finished, he shot off along the trail.

Princess nodded her head and pranced, and with a swish of her glittering white mane she galloped through the air after him. The other Little Sparkles followed, like a tiny glimmering rainbow. They whirled and looped through the air, past the teacups and the carousel, and ducked in between the dodgem cars. Holly and Rose raced after them.

The trail of sticky footprints stopped at the sandpit next to the log flume.

"Those scallywags!" Holly gasped.

The two Poopers were scratching at the sand with their stubby fingers as they tried to cover up something. The first one still had the cupcake case stuck to his head, but now the chocolate icing was mixed with sand. Sand was all over the second Pooper's flabby grey skin, too, like dirt stuck to old chewing gum.

"They've buried Hari's present!" Rose cried.

The Poopers looked up and scowled horribly at the girls and the Little Sparkles.

"We pooped the present!" one of the Poopers shouted. "We're super duper Pirate Party Poopers!"

The other Pooper chanted:

"Umpitty bumpitty, yippedy yee!
What will we poop next?
Just wait and see!"

With a yip, Peppy leapt into the sandpit and began scrabbling at the mound of sand with his front and back paws. There was a tiny, gurgling bunny giggle and Bubbles joined in, burrowing. They worked so fast that there was a dazzling haze of glitter over the sandpit.

Holly and Rose knelt down and scooped
away handfuls of sand.

"Yo-ho-ho! We've found the pirate's
treasure!" Rose joked as Peppy dug out
Hari's present. It was still in its wrapping

paper. Holly picked it up and brushed off the sand until it was as good as new.

"Now, where have those flubbery Poopers gone?" she asked, shading her eyes with her hand and staring around the Adventure Park. Rose did the same.

"There's no sign of the Pooper with the cupcake case on his head," Rose said. "But the other one is over there!" She pointed to a sign saying "Log Flume".

The girls raced over to it. A group of excited children were about to get into what looked like a hollowed-out log floating on an artificial river. The Pooper was at the front of the queue. He stuck out his tongue at Holly and Rose as he hopped in the narrow boat.

The twins looked at each other in dismay.

"He'll poop the log flume!" Holly gasped. "The Poopers aren't just going to spoil Hari's party – they going to poop the entire park!"

4

Trouble on Board

There was no time to lose. Holly and
Rose stashed Hari's present under the
counter at the entrance to the ride and
jumped into the front of a log boat. It
was packed with children sitting one in
front of the other on little wooden
benches. Rose sat down in front of
Holly and the Little Sparkles fluttered
on to their Pirate Hats.

Holly tapped Rose on the shoulder.

"Keep an eye out for the Pooper. If he poops the log flume, it could be dangerous!"

The ride began to move along the narrow waterway. It felt very wobbly.

The little boy in front of Rose turned round.

"It's not supposed to rock like this,"

he said nervously.

"It's the Pooper," Holly hissed, pointing ahead.

At the front of the boat, invisible to all the other passengers on the ride, the flabby grey Pooper was  hopping up and down, first on one side, then the other, making the boat lurch about. Sand flew from his fur as he moved.

"He's trying to sink us!" Rose gasped, clutching hold of the sides as the log boat whizzed along faster and faster in the foaming white water. Water began to puddle around their feet.

"Stop him jumping about!" Peppy yipped.

The Little Sparkles whizzed towards the Pooper. Tiny rainbows of light glimmered in the misty spray around the front of the boat as they tried to get close to the Pooper.

"It's too splashy!" Holly said as the Little Sparkles darted in and out of the haze.

The Pooper stuck out his tongue. Now that the sand had washed off him, he looked like a mouldy old lump of bread. He launched himself into the air and landed with a soggy squelch on the edge of the boat.

"Eek!" The passengers screamed as the log boat rocked wildly, causing a wave of water to wash over everyone.

There was a flash of rainbow light as the Little Sparkles were swept away in the torrent.

"Oh no! Will they be OK?" Holly asked worriedly.

"It looks like they are," Rose reassured her, pointing to the shimmering lights that had reappeared in the mist.

"EEK!" There was a louder scream from the passengers as an even bigger wave washed over the ride.

"Oh no, he's scaring the other passengers. I've got an idea how to stop him..." Rose took off her pirate hat and bent forward until the ends of her plaits almost touched the foaming water beneath the rocking boat. She grabbed hold of the side with one hand to steady herself. Then, slowly and carefully, she stretched out her hat towards the Pooper to try to trap him.

SWISH!

Rose swept her hat towards the Pooper, but he saw it coming and leapt clear. At that exact moment, the log boat hit a bend in the ride. It tipped on to its side and Rose fell backwards. She landed in the puddle of water in the bottom of the boat.

Holly helped her up. "Are you all right?"

"I'm fine," Rose spluttered. "Look!" She pointed behind them.

The Pooper was teetering on the edge of the boat. As the log boat whizzed round the corner, he flew off it, right over the fence and out of the Adventure Park!

Everyone on the log boat sighed with relief as it stopped rocking. Five damp Little Sparkles fluttered down into the boat and hovered between Rose and Holly. They shook their fur and began to twinkle again as the log flume ride came safely to a halt.

"Shame we didn't get the chance to turn that Pooper into a Little Sparkle," Holly said as they stepped off the boat, wiping damp glitter out of their eyes.

"At least he won't be able to poop Hari's party any more," Rose pointed out, retrieving the present from under the counter.

As they made their way back to the

Jolly Roger, their pirate outfits begin to dry out in the warm sunshine.

"What's the other Pooper been up to while we were all on the ride?" Rose wondered.

Holly squeezed the last of the water droplets from her long toffee-coloured plaits. "We'd better find out," she said, "before he can do any more pooping!"

5

Poop Goes the Party!

The twins stared in horror at the Jolly Roger. It was in a terrible state. The Little Sparkles jingle-jangled in dismay.

"It's worse than I imagined," Rose groaned.

The Jolly Roger's mast was bent and the net climbing frame that led to the crow's nest was in tatters. The barrel was on its side and sticky lemonade had sloshed all over the table and the deck.

Hari's mum and the party guests stood open-mouthed as they watched the Jolly Roger's sail, the flag with the skull and crossbones, and the strings of red and black party flags fall slowly to the floor in a horrid tangle.

Hari looked as if he might cry.

"Come on, everyone," Hari's mum announced. "We can go on another ride. I'll come back later and clear up this mess."

"The log boat was – er, looks – really fun," Holly said. Rose nodded.

"That's a great ride for pirates," Hari agreed, looking a bit more cheerful. "Abandon ship, me hearties! Take to the boats!"

"Aye, aye, Captain!" Jenny, Billy, Maisie and the other party guests yelled. The twins ducked around the back of the ship while everyone else raced towards the log boat ride.

When the coast was clear, Holly and Rose hurried up the rope bridge. The deck of the Jolly Roger looked like a storm had washed over it. Pineapple, cheese chunks and plastic palm trees were floating in puddles of lemonade. The treasure chest cake was so soggy it looked as if it had sunk to the bottom of the ocean. The coins and sweetie-necklaces that decorated it were all over the floor. Presents were scattered everywhere.

"It's a wreck!" Holly sighed.

"There's no time to tidy up now," said Rose. "We've got to find the Pooper before he does even more damage."

There was a sound like faraway bells as the Little Sparkles hovered above them, singing softly to each other in tiny sweet-sounding voices:

"We must find that naughty Pooper,
And make Hari's party super!"

The Jolly Roger was showered in twinkly light as Peppy, Tikki, Princess and Bubble fanned out to search the deck.

"I shall check the treasure chest cake," volunteered Tubbs. A moment later he reported back to the twins.

"The Party Pooper isn't in the cake!" he mumbled with his mouth full of sweetie-necklace.

"Shh!" Rose put her fingers to her lips as she carefully put down Hari's present. "I can hear noises under the deck."

Holly and Rose lay down and put their ears to the ground.

"Something's moving about down there," Holly said. "It must be the Pooper!"

They crept quietly down the stairs, followed closely by the Little Sparkles. The twins shivered. It was dim and spooky down below. There were no windows, only small portholes.

"We need some more light," Rose murmured.

In an instant, the hold of the ship lit up with what looked like tiny stars as the Little Sparkles glowed in the darkness.

"That's much better, thanks!" Holly said.

The twins and the Little Sparkles looked cautiously around. The hold was stacked with lemonade barrels like the one on deck.

Tikki the kitten glittered like gold and began to sing softly:

"In the corner,
over there,
Something's
moving – please take care."

Rose caught a glimpse of a shape moving through the shadows. A shape with a cupcake case stuck to it...

"The Pooper's behind the lemonade barrel by that porthole!" Rose whispered. She, Holly and the Little Sparkles edged towards him.

The Pooper hopped up on the end of what looked like a big black pipe pointing out of the porthole.

Princess the pony neighed nervously.

"It's a big gun called a cannon." Holly told her as the Pooper jumped back into the shadows. "There's one at every porthole. Don't worry, they're only pretend. They can't hurt any—"

POP!

The Little Sparkles jumped in fright and their glittering lights went out.

"Cannon fire!" Tubbs yelled, pulling his green head, legs and tail into his rainbow shell. "Take cover!"

6

Patching Up a Pooper

POP! POP! POP!

Rose and Holly covered their heads
with their arms and stared nervously
through the
shadows. The
Pooper was
releasing
the tops of
the lemonade
barrels.

"It's only the barrel lids that are making the noise!" Holly exclaimed. "The Pooper's taking them off to make the lemonade go flat."

There was a happy tinkling as the Little Sparkles sighed in relief. They began to glimmer again, and soon the hold of the ship looked as if it were lit with beautiful fairy lights.

There was the loudest POP of all as another lid flew off.

"*OWWWW!*" yelled the Pooper, clutching his head.

"The lid hit him!" Rose said in horror.

The twins hurried over to the Pooper. He was sitting in a crumpled heap on the ground, still wearing the cupcake-case hat.

"It stings!" he groaned.

"Are you OK?" Rose asked. "Let me see!"

"Poopers don't need help from silly girls!" the Pooper muttered, taking his hand away from his head. There was a little dent in the wrinkly grey skin just above his eye.

"You're going to need a bandage," Holly declared. She untied a red and black ribbon from one of her plaits and handed it to him.

The Pooper took it reluctantly and began to wrap it around his head.

"Now we've got the Pooper cornered, maybe we can get him to have some fun!" Rose whispered. "Then he'll turn into a brand new Little Sparkle!"

The Pooper had bandaged his head so the ribbon covered his eye, just like a pirate eyepatch.

"Shan't stop pooping the party just because you were nice!" he said, sticking out his tongue. "Ner, ner!" he shouted over his shoulder as he bounced up the steps.

"Stop him! We have to make him have fun!" Holly cried.

The twins and the Little Sparkles zoomed after the Pooper into the bright sunshine on deck.

He had jumped up on to the food table again. When he saw them coming he grabbed one of the plastic cutlasses from the cheese and pineapple.

"On guard!" the Pooper shouted, brandishing the tiny cutlass at the girls and the Little Sparkles.

"Look at him," Rose gasped. "The cupcake case looks just like a pirate hat, and he's wearing an eyepatch and holding a cutlass. There's even a parrot balloon floating above him. He's a proper little pirate!"

Holly grinned. "And I know just how we can get a Pirate Pooper to have fun!"

7

Party Pooper Pirate

Rose and the Little Sparkles gathered around Holly.

"Everyone pretend the Pooper is a real pirate," Rose whispered. They all nodded, then turned around to face the Pooper.

"Help, help!" Holly cried in pretend terror, making her knees knock together. "The Perilous Pirate Pooper has come to plunder our ship!"

"Oh, oh, oh!" squeaked Rose in mock alarm, waving her arms in the air.

"Arrr!" snarled the Pooper.

Bubbles flattened her ears and Tubbs ducked inside his shell. The other Little Sparkles fluttered around in fake panic.

"Neeeeiiigh!" whinnied Princess, pawing her hooves.

"Miaow!" squealed Tikki, making her whiskers quiver.

"Yip!" Peppy yapped, putting his tail between his legs.

They were all brilliant at pretending to be scared. The Pooper looked very pleased with himself.

"Time to walk the plank!" he shouted, waving the little plastic cutlass.

"No! No!" the twins and the Little Sparkles squealed, backing on to the

wooden beam.

The Pooper grinned. "Ner, ner! Can't stop me, you cowardly landlubbers!"

"Our plan's working!" Rose murmured as she, Holly and the Little Sparkles stood fake-trembling at the end of the plank.

The Pooper was beaming from podgy ear to podgy ear. "No one can beat the Perilous Pirate Pooper!" he laughed.

Then Holly stopped pretending to be scared and put her hands on her hips. The Pooper looked at her in surprise.

"It's fun playing pirates, isn't it?" Holly asked.

"Yes!" agreed the Pooper, a little reluctantly. He waved his cutlass. "Yes,"

he said more confidently. "YES! It's really, really FUN!"

There was a PUFF! of glitter, and in place of the Pooper stood a very pretty parrot with bright green feathers.

"We did it," cried Rose. "He's a Little Sparkle now!"

8

Animal Magic

There was a tinkling noise and a shower of emerald glitter as the parrot flapped his wings. "Look at my lovely new feathers!" he squawked happily.

"Yip!" Peppy's tail wagged and wagged as he took a shiny gold balloon out of his party bag. He gave it to the parrot to hold in his beak.

"It's magic," Holly whispered as the balloon filled with air.

"Sparkle magic," Rose agreed.

The five Little Sparkles formed a ring around the parrot and sang in their sweet little voices:

"Spread the lovely party joy to every
little girl and boy,
No more a grumpy Party Pooper,
make the parties super duper."

The balloon and the parrot floated gently into the air. The twins watched as the new Little Sparkle waved with one of his wings, then soared up and away over the Adventure Park, until he was a distant speck in the sky.

"Now he can make parties fun instead of trying to ruin them," Rose declared happily as the Little Sparkles danced for joy.

"But we still have to fix the Jolly Roger," Holly reminded them. "Hari and the others might come back at any moment!"

The twins raced on to the deck and began to pick up the scattered presents. The Little Sparkles took out their party bags and zoomed around the Jolly Roger in a haze of glitter.

SPOOSH! There was a burst of magical hundreds-and-thousands over the food table, and in an instant, the party food was the same delicious spread it had been before.

"Do you think anyone will notice there's a sweetie-necklace missing from the inside of the treasure chest?" Rose whispered to Holly.

"I don't think anyone will mind," she replied. "And Tubbs has already eaten half of it!"

They giggled and looked for the little turtle. He was floating up to the crow's nest with the other Little Sparkles, munching on the necklace.

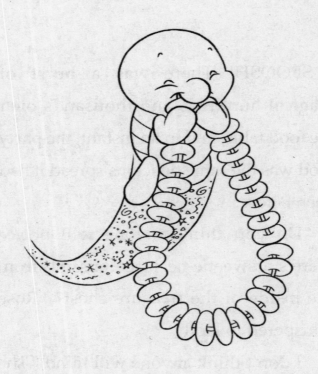

The next moment – SWOOSH! – Hundreds-and-thousands sprinkled down from the crows nest. In a flash, the sail, the netting and the flags were magically mended, and the sticky lemonade mess was all cleaned up.

Then the Little Sparkles took out their matching party blowers. They floated in the air above the ship, looking like a small sparkly cloud. Then, all together, they blew: TOOO-OOOT!

At the sound, the Jolly Roger swayed gently.

"The Little Sparkles did it again!" Holly said.

Now that their job was done, the five magical little creatures waved and floated away in a blaze of glitter – over the heads of the pirate party guests, who were returning to the ship.

"See you soon," the girls called as they waved goodbye.

"Ahoy there!" Hari yelled, waving back.

For a heart-stopping moment, Holly thought he'd somehow seen the Little Sparkles, and knew their secret.

"It's OK; Hari thinks we're waving to him!" Rose whispered.

"Ahoy there, me hearties!" called Holly. "The ship's moving again!"

Hari dashed up the rope bridge on to the deck, closely followed by his mum, Jenny, Billy, Maisie and the other guests.

"Wow!" Hari sounded awestruck as he looked around the Jolly Roger. "Someone's made my pirate party perfect!" He beamed from ear to ear. "It must be magic!"

Holly and Rose looked at each other and shared a secret smile.

"Parties are magic!" they agreed.

Don't miss the other
books in the series!

Little Sparkles

Party at the Zoo

Have fun with these tiny magical animals!

Emily Moon

Little Sparkles

Party in the Castle

Have fun with these tiny magical animals!

Emily Moon